THE INCREDIBLE DINOSAUR EXPEDITION

Karen Dolby

Illustrated by Brenda Haw
Cover illustration: Luis Rey and Brenda Haw

Designed by Patrick Knowles
Cover design: Russell Punter

Series editor: Gaby Waters

Contents

About this Book

The Incredible Dinosaur Expedition is an exciting adventure story with a difference. The difference is that you can take part in the adventure.

Throughout the book, there are tricky puzzles and perplexing problems to solve. You will need to find the answers to understand the next episode in the story.

Look at the pictures carefully and watch out for vital clues and information. Sometimes you will need to flick back through the book to help you find an answer.

There are extra clues on page 43 and you can check your answers on pages 44 to 48.

Just turn the page to begin the adventure…

The Dinosaur Discovery

Freddie was bored, so bored that he had even lent Jo his roller skates. He munched his way through a bumper bag of banana toffees and wished that something exciting would happen.

Just then, Freddie's friend, Zack, zoomed up on his skateboard.

"Come and read this," Zack yelled, waving a very crumpled newspaper page.

"But newspapers are so boring," Freddie groaned, aiming a toffee at Zack's head.

"There's been the most amazing dinosaur discovery," said Zack, ignoring Freddie.

"And it's near here," Jo exclaimed, staring at the page. "In Fossilwood Forest."

"Let's go," said Zack. "Maybe WE can find some dinosaur bones."

Freddie groaned again and carried on munching. But two toffees later he set off after Zack and Jo.

On the right you can read Zack's newspaper.

Zack

Jo

Freddie

~DAILY SCOOP~

AMAZING DINOSAUR DISCOVERY
...it's a monster mystery

by Ivor Lead

Late last night, the most incredible dinosaur discovery EVER was made in Fossilwood Forest.

A team of dinosaur experts led by Professor Cuthbert Crank-Pott have found a whole dinosaur skeleton, of a type never seen before.

MONSTERMAGUS

Professor Crank-Pott has named this amazing dinosaur MONSTERMAGUS. In an exclusive interview earlier today, he described the monster.

"This dinosaur was huge – 15 metres tall with large, sharp claws on its feet. It must have devoured enormous amounts of flesh every day and makes Tyrannosaurus Rex look as fierce as a baby hamster."

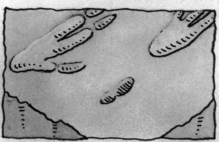

These amazing fossil footprints were found beneath the dinosaur skeleton. The large prints belong to the Monstermagus, but the little one is a mystery. It looks like a human shoeprint.

Humans and dinosaurs never lived on earth together . . . or did they?

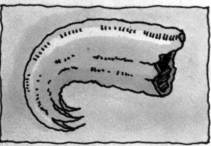

This three-spiked claw belonged to the Monstermagus. It had two of them, one on each of its feet. Experts believe they were used for spearing its prey. So far only one of them has been found.

MYSTERIOUS CLAIMS

On top of his startling skeleton discovery, Professor Crank-Pott claims that he has found a method of hatching live dinosaurs from prehistoric eggs!

He refuses to reveal the secret of his discovery but promises to show the world the results.

Is this really possible? No one knows for sure. A rival expert, Dr Noel Knowall says the Professor's claims are "crazy" "daft" "mad" and "impossible". We shall have to wait and see . . .

Professor Crank-Pott

FOSSILWOOD FOREST LONG AGO

150 million years ago, dinosaurs roamed what is now Fossilwood Forest. No one knows what the landscape looked like then. Some experts say it was a marshy swamp, others think the land was dotted with erupting volcanoes. The Monstermagus and the footprint fossils were buried in a layer of volcanic lava, but nearby, experts have found fossils of shells and prehistoric crocodiles.

In Fossilwood Forest

Half an hour later they stumbled into a clearing in Fossilwood Forest. This was the site of the dinosaur discovery, but it wasn't at all what they expected.

"It looks just like a rubbish dump," moaned Freddie.

Zack and Jo pulled out their spades and started searching through the rubbish for dinosaur bones. Freddie found a comfortable spot beneath a tree and pulled out something plastic and stripey.

"What's that?" cried Zack.

"My inflatable air cushion, of course," said Freddie.

Then, to Zack and Jo's amazement, he blew up the air cushion and sat down with his pocket dinosaur book and a mammoth bar of chocolate.

Jo chucked a slithery earthworm in Freddie's direction and carried on scrabbling in the rubbish. All of a sudden, she spotted something.

"Look! Look over there," she cried in an excited voice. "It's the Monstermagus claw!"

Can you find the missing Monstermagus claw?

Lost in the Woods

Very carefully, Jo prised the claw out of the ground. She wrapped it in Freddie's empty toffee bag and put it in her rucksack.

"Let's go home," Freddie said as a raindrop trickled down his neck. "I'm getting wet and this wood is starting to give me the creeps."

The other two agreed. They had to make their way to Forest Lane. But which way was it?

"I know," said Jo. "Take the left fork at the well and . . ."

"No," said Zack. "It's straight on at the well and across the crossroads. First left, first right, right again and first left. Over the bridge and we're there. Easy."

"Wrong," said Jo. "Left at the well and straight on at Hangman's Cross. Follow the path round past the track to Spring Cottage, turn left at the end and take the second path on the right. Then follow the long, wiggly path to Forest Lane."

Forest Lane

Forest Wall

Spring Cottage

Hangman's Cross

Tombstones

"You're both wrong," said Freddie. "We go right at Hangman's Cross, follow the path over the bridge, turn second left, then first left and Forest Lane is at the end."

They chose Zack's route and as they walked on through the forest the sky grew darker.

Where does Zack's route take them?
Whose route is correct?

8

St Elmo's Church

Lizard Rock

Stony Brook

Ruined Cottage

Wild Woods

Marlpit

Stone Barn

Old Well

Haunted House

Dinosaurs!

All of a sudden they saw a patch of bright light ahead. They hurried towards it and stepped out into hot, hazy sunshine.

Jo stared in amazement. The forest had become a jungle. A giant dragonfly whizzed past Zack's nose and Freddie shrieked as a large, slimy slug slid over his shoes.

But most terrifying of all, were the strange roars and crashes, coming closer and closer. Zack made a gap in the leaves and peered through.

"M . . . m . . . monsters," he gasped.

"No, dinosaurs," gulped Freddie. "Or what look like dinosaurs."

"But . . . how . . ?" Jo began.

Some of the dinosaurs were so near they could hear them chewing. Were THEY going to be eaten next?

"It's all right!" said Freddie, pulling his dinosaur book out of his pocket. "Look, it says here that some dinosaurs only eat plants. They're quite safe. But we must look out for the meat-eaters."

You can see Freddie's dinosaur book over the page.
Can you work out which dinosaurs eat meat and which eat plants?

Freddie's Book

Dinosaurs

Dinosaurs were a group of creatures who lived on earth for 135 million years. They died out over 60 million years before man appeared.

The word dinosaur means "terrible lizard". There were lots of different types of dinosaurs and we know what they looked like from fossils, although we don't know what colour they were.

Tyrannosaurus Rex

Fossils

A fossil is the remains of an animal or plant preserved in stone. There are fossils of dinosaur bones, eggs, teeth and claws. There are even fossils of their footprints and skin.

A dinosaur became a fossil if its body was buried quickly. This was most likely to happen if it died near water. You can find out how this happened below.

How Fossils Were Made

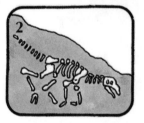

When a dinosaur died near a swamp or river its body sank into the mud at the bottom. There its flesh rotted away, leaving the skeleton.

Layers of mud, sand and gravel built up. Then chemicals from the water entered the dinosaur's bones, slowly turning the skeleton into rock.

Movements in the earth's crust shift rocks containing fossils to the surface. Wind and rain wear away the rock and uncover part of the fossil.

Footprints

Megalosaurus

Fossil footprints were made when a dinosaur walked on mud which was baked hard by the sun and covered by sand. Slowly this turned into rock with the footprint tracks still in it.

What Dinosaurs Ate

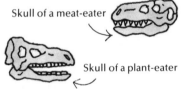
Skull of a meat-eater

Skull of a plant-eater

Some dinosaurs ate meat – they had sharp, pointed teeth. Others ate plants – they had flat, grinding teeth and some had bony beaks.

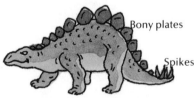
Bony plates

Spikes

Plant-eaters had to protect themselves from meat-eaters. Some plant-eaters had spikes or bony plates on their bodies, others stayed in herds.

Big and Small

Diplodocus

Compsognathus

Diplodocus was one of the biggest dinosaurs, measuring 28 metres from its head to the tip of its tail. It ate plants and stayed in herds.

The smallest dinosaur, called *Compsognathus,* was only the size of a crow. It ran very fast and ate insects and small reptiles.

Baby Dinosaurs

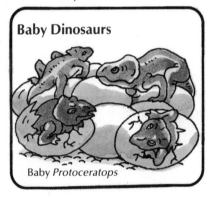
Baby *Protoceratops*

Most dinosaurs laid eggs. These were buried, or laid in a hollow "nest" in the ground. Fossils of *Protoceratops* eggs, like the ones above, have been found with baby dinosaur bones inside. The babies looked just like small adults.

13

Follow the Footprints

Zack and Jo didn't wait to look at Freddie's dinosaur book. They turned round and ran back through the bushes, retracing their steps. Freddie followed. Their footprints were clear enough, but everything else was different. Where were they?

"We must have walked through a time warp," Freddie said cheerfully.

"WHAT?" cried Zack and Jo together.

"I think we've travelled backwards in time . . . to the age of the dinosaurs," Freddie explained.

"But they're the wrong colour for dinosaurs," said Jo.

"How do you know?" asked Freddie.

They walked on in silence. Zack and Jo tried hard to find another explanation, but they couldn't think of one.

"But how did it happen?" asked Jo. "I don't understand. What did we do?"

No one knew. Jo stopped suddenly. There was something odd about the tracks on the ground.

What has Jo seen?

Scraps of Paper

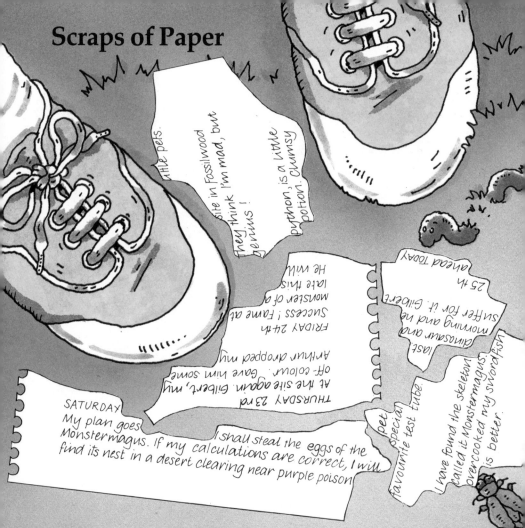

Further on in the jungle, Freddie noticed some torn-up scraps of paper lying in the grass. Each one was covered in black, spidery writing. He picked them up and pieced them together like a jigsaw puzzle.

"It's a page from somebody's diary," Jo exclaimed.

"And whoever wrote it is here with us now," added Zack, looking at the bottom of the page. "The last date is August 25th. That's today."

Piece together the scraps of paper to find out what is written in the diary.

16

17

Hands Up

Freddie was worried. Whoever wrote the diary had some very weird ideas.

"I think we should watch out," he said.

"So you should," answered a sinister voice. "Hands up!"

They looked up – straight into the barrel of a shot gun. At the other end was a white-haired man wearing a bow tie.

"What are you doing here?" demanded the man. "That's MY diary and you've walked through MY time door."

Then he shouted at the miserable-looking boy standing beside him. Jo gasped in surprise. It was Arthur, star of the school science club.

"It's all your fault Arthur," yelled the man. "Tie these spies up at once."

Arthur looked even more miserable, but he did as he was told. Jo tried to speak to him, but he wouldn't look at her.

The man prodded Freddie in the back with the barrel of his gun and ordered them to move. He marched them along at break-neck speed, deeper and deeper into the thick, tropical jungle. Curious eyes stared out at them from the undergrowth.

Large drops of rain splashed down and mud squelched under their feet. But still they walked on . . . and on.

Zack glanced back at the man. His face was very familiar. He was sure he had seen him before.

Do you know who the man is? What is his name?

Prisoners Underground

The Professor stopped suddenly. Ahead lay a large hole in the ground.

"Stop!" barked the Professor. "This is the end of the road for you three meddlesome brats."

He dragged Zack by the scruff of his neck and pushed him down into the hole. Then he grabbed Jo.

"Down you go," he sneered. "You should make very interesting fossils."

When Freddie's turn came something strange happened. The Professor turned away for a split second and Arthur thrust a scrap of paper into his hand. But there was no time to look at it. Freddie skidded down the hole and along a dark, wet tunnel. Then he felt himself falling down and down into the darkness.

He landed on a mound of soft earth, next to Zack and Jo. They were sitting in a shadowy, underground cave. It was cold, dark and wet. What were they going to do?

Freddie unfolded Arthur's note. He wanted to help them! But first they had to find a way out of the cave. Zack tried climbing up to the tunnel, but he was pushed back by a stream of water pouring into the cave. There was a hole in the roof, but it was too high to reach.

By now, the tunnel stream had become a torrent and water was splashing around their ankles . . . and their knees. They had to find a way out FAST or they would drown.

In a flash of inspiration, Freddie realized he had something that would save their lives and help them to escape from the cave.

How can they escape?

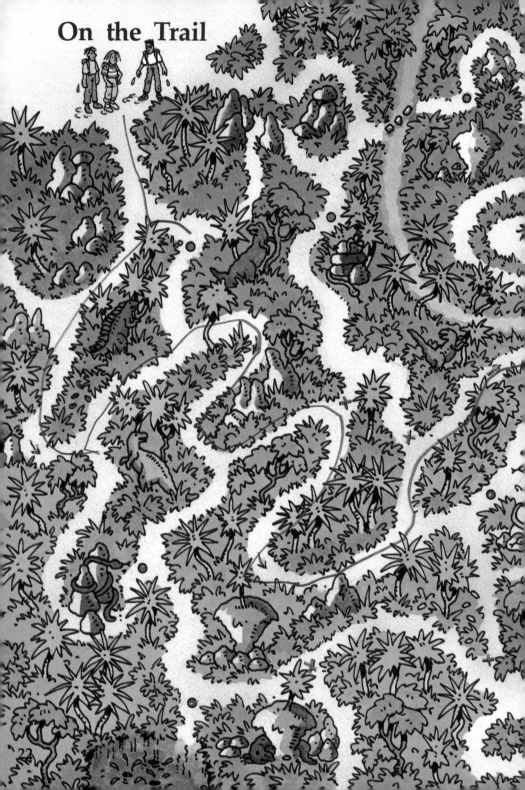

On the Trail

They scrambled up out of the flooded cave into a clearing in the jungle. The rain had stopped and their clothes began to dry in the sunshine. They looked around for Arthur's trail.

"Can we trust him?" asked Zack uncertainly.

They had no choice. Arthur was the only one who could lead them to the Professor. And without the Professor, there was no chance of getting home.

"I'm starving," groaned Freddie opening a packet of banana custard biscuits.

Jo pulled a face at Freddie, but Zack took no notice. His eyes scanned the ground. He set off along a narrow track leading deep into the jungle. A little way on, he spotted three twigs in the shape of an arrow. It was the start of Arthur's trail.

Can you follow Arthur's trail through the jungle?

Flying Monsters

At the edge of the jungle, they heard a loud wooshing noise. All around, the trees began to rustle. They looked up and saw an enormous flying dinosaur.

"It's a Pteranodon," said Freddie in a know-all voice.

The Pteranodon swooped down and seized Jo and Freddie in its sharp claws. Then it opened its beak and grabbed Zack by his collar. It soared above the jungle, away from the trail, and dropped them on a high rocky crag.

"I think we're next on the menu," Zack gulped.

But just as the dinosaur opened its giant beak, a shadow fell across the rock. An even bigger monster appeared in the sky flying towards them.

"It's a Quetzalcoatlus!" shrieked Freddie.

It dived, screeching, at the Pteranodon and the two monsters flew into battle. Jo crossed her fingers and shut her eyes tight . . .

When she opened them again, the monsters had gone. They were safe, but they had lost Arthur's trail. How would they find the Professor and the Monstermagus nest now?

Zack had an idea. He pulled out his pocket compass. North was directly behind him.

Where is the nest?

A Dangerous Descent

First they had to climb down the mountain. The ground seemed a very long way off. Below them was a series of strange pillar rocks.

"We can jump from one rock to the next and climb over the tree," said Freddie. "But there are some terrible things in the way."

There were poisonous snakes and vapour pools, dangerous rubble and spiky bushes, a bubbling stream of red-hot lava . . . and dinosaurs.

"Follow me," said Zack leaping onto the first pillar.

Can you find a safe route down the rockface, dodging all the obstacles?

27

Journey through the Jungle

Keeping the blue-capped volcano in sight, they headed off through the unknown jungle. All around, they could hear strange noises and rustlings. They stopped abruptly. Straight ahead, was a dinosaur the size of an elephant.

"It's an Allosaurus," said Freddie, cheerfully. "Where's my camera? Imagine him next to Dad in my photo album."

Neither Zack nor Jo wanted to hang about taking photos. They turned and dashed away. Freddie followed . . . and so did the Allosaurus.

They ran at full pelt until they were ready to drop, but the dinosaur showed no signs of slowing up. Suddenly Zack stopped under a tall tree. He jumped up, grabbed a sturdy branch and hauled himself up. Jo and Freddie did the same.

Yoa urv ern yeat rhn
eesd. Ton'w torra ybout
thm eonstermagut.
Shp erofessor'd sarw
tilp lui tt ts oleef poo
rnh eouy. Roc uaf nint
dht eimd eooro st nhp
erofessor't simc
ehari — tt'a so nlt,
dorr nolo lp fapet
riew dito hnr eer
dibbon.

Perched up high among the leaves, they felt safe. The Allosaurus paused below them and looked up. It snarled and gnashed its teeth, but it couldn't reach them.

At last it walked on. They waited until it was out of sight before climbing back down to the ground. Then Jo spotted the crumpled piece of paper pinned to a tree trunk.

"We must be back on Arthur's trail," she cried excitedly.

Jo unpinned the paper and groaned. The message was in code.

"I can't work it out at all," she said. "You two have a look."

Can you decode Arthur's message?

At the Nest

They crept on. It wasn't far now. The clearing lay straight ahead and in the distance, they could see the steaming poison pools.

All of a sudden, Zack saw the Professor. He was standing in a hollow beside eight large, white eggs. Behind him lay an enormous, sleeping dinosaur. It was the Monstermagus.

They ducked behind a boulder and watched the Professor lift the eggs out of the nest. He examined them one by one.

"He's stealing the eggs," gasped Freddie. "We've got to stop him."

But there was nothing they could do. The Professor laid the eggs in a large metal chest, closed the lid and tapped some buttons on the top. Then he called to Arthur and marched off briskly towards the blue-capped volcano carrying only a camera and tripod.

"It's our big chance," said Zack. "Quickly! Let's take the eggs."

If they replaced the eggs with stones, the Professor would never know they were gone. But there was one problem. The box was locked.

"It's a combination lock," said Jo, looking at the buttons on the lid. "You press certain buttons in a special order to unlock it."

Some buttons were numbered, others were blank. Which ones should they press?

Then Freddie noticed a scrap of paper lying beside the metal chest. There was a list of confusing instructions written on it.

"These might help," he said, reading the first one aloud.

Which buttons should they press to open the box? You will need to find the missing numbers first.

Each row and diagonal adds up to 15.

The buttons are numbered 1 to 9.

Press the evens to open and the odds to close, in ascending order.

The Professor's Papers

Freddie carefully lifted the eggs out of the chest and Zack carried them back to the nest. The Monstermagus was still sleeping peacefully. Jo filled the chest with stones and locked it again.

"Now we've got to find the Professor's time chart," she said.

Freddie started emptying the Professor's bags onto the ground. There were hundreds of maps and papers. But which one was the time chart? They had to find it fast. The Professor could return at any moment.

Can you find the time chart?

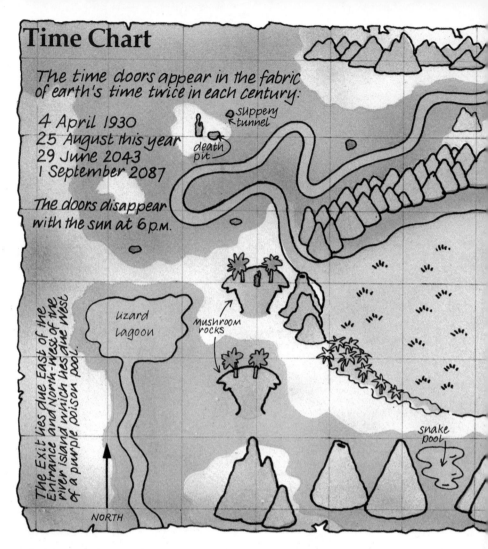

Time Chart

The time doors appear in the fabric of earth's time twice in each century:

4 April 1930
25 August this year
29 June 2043
1 September 2087

The doors disappear with the sun at 6 p.m.

The Exit lies due East of the Entrance and North-west of the river island which lies due West of a purple poison pool.

slippery tunnel

death pit

lizard lagoon

mushroom rocks

snake pool

NORTH

Zack untied the red ribbon and carefully unrolled the tattered, old chart. He spread it out on the ground in front of them.

"It's a map of the whole area," Jo exclaimed. "The Professor must have been here before."

Zack, Jo and Freddie stared blankly at the map. They were stumped. The nest was marked with an arrow. But where was the time door? It wasn't shown anywhere.

"This is hopeless," Freddie wailed. "We'll never find our way home."

There are two time doors an Entrance and an Exit. Both appear as a hole through which the past or future can be seen.

The Entrance lies due East of the death pit and North-East of the tree stump on the mushroom rock.

mushroom rock

pillar rocks

crocodile swamp

swamp island

lava pool

river islands

purple-poison pools

blue-capped volcano

nest

Jo was about to agree when she started reading the strange, spidery notes scrawled at the sides of the map.

"I think these are clues," she explained, pointing at the notes. "If we work out the compass bearings, we can find the time door."

Jo studied the map while Zack and Freddie kept watch.

"I've found it," Jo said.

... Just in time. The Professor was returning. Quickly, they dived for cover.

Can you find the time door?

Crocodile Swamp

The Professor stared in horror at the mess. Papers and maps lay everywhere.

"Run for it," Zack yelled, sprinting towards the jungle.

Too late. The Professor spotted them at once and started off in hot pursuit.

Zack, Jo and Freddie ran on and on as fast as they could, until they came to the edge of a vast, steamy swamp.

"We've got to cross this swamp," said Zack. "It's the quickest way to the time door."

"We can use that hollow tree trunk as a canoe," said a voice.

It was Arthur! He had escaped from the Professor. Jo and Freddie scrambled into the trunk, as Zack and Arthur pushed them out into the swamp. But what could they use as paddles?

"We can't use our hands," said Arthur. "Look at those crocodiles!"

He was right. Then Jo realized she and Zack both had something they could use.

What can they use as paddles?

Freddie and the Monstermagus

At the other side, the swamp was surrounded by a wall of steep mountains and volcanoes. There was only one way through – a narrow, muddy pass at the foot of a smoking volcano. A stream of red-hot lava was starting to pour down the side of the volcano towards the pass.

They dashed to the pass, ran under a rocky ledge and on to safety. But where was Freddie? They looked back. He was still a long way off, paddling in the water. And there behind him was . . . a huge Monstermagus.

"What can we do? What's going to happen?" wailed Jo.

Ledge

"It's obvious," said Arthur, tapping his calculator keys.

Zack and Jo looked blank, so Arthur explained.

"The lava is heading for that ledge. Freddie has to run eight metres to pass under its midpoint and he does 100 metres in 25 seconds."

"The lava flows two metres in a second. It's six metres above the ledge which is 17 metres from the ground. The Monstermagus is 16 metres behind Freddie, runs six metres a second and we already know how tall it is."

Can you work out what happens?

39

Looking for the Time Door

They clambered on up through the pass until they came out into open ground. They could see jungle just a little way ahead. The time door was here somewhere . . .

Freddie stopped shaking and began grumbling.

"I was nearly eaten and it's all your fault, Zack," he muttered. "This expedition was your idea. I was quite happy being bored at home."

But no one was taking any notice. They were running out of time.

Zack unrolled the Professor's chart. There were now only minutes left before the time door disappeared. They HAD to find it.

"We're in the right place," said Zack. "But where's the door?"

"We have to look for it," said Arthur. "It should be easy to see."

They paced up and down searching. Suddenly they spotted it!

Where is the time door?

The Footprint Fossil

Back in their own time, it was hard to believe it had ever happened. Fossilwood Forest was as dark and gloomy as ever and even the Professor looked less crazy.

From behind a bush, they watched as the Professor struggled through the forest with his precious chest. What would he do when he realized it was full of stones? What would he say when he discovered Arthur had taken the film out of his camera?

The next day, they took the Monstermagus claw and a few prehistoric shells to the museum. The first thing they saw was the famous footprints fossil. They gazed at the small human shoeprint.

"You know who made it don't you?" Jo laughed.

"No one would believe us if we tried to explain!" said Zack.

Do you know who made the fossil footprint?

Clues

Pages 6-7
You can see what the claw looks like in Zack's newspaper on page 5.

Pages 8-9
This is easy. First follow Zack's route to find out where it takes them. Then follow Jo's and Freddie's routes in turn.

Pages 10-11
Freddie's dinosaur book on pages 12 and 13 makes this easy.

Pages 14-15
Work out which are Zack, Jo and Freddie's footprints. Are there any others?

Pages 16-17
Trace each piece of paper, or photocopy the page and cut out the pieces. Match them up and stick them together to read the diary.

Pages 18-19
Look back at Zack's newspaper on page 5.

Pages 20-21
What does Freddie have with him? Look at pages 6 and 7.

Pages 22-23
You don't need a clue for this. Use your eyes.

Pages 24-25
Arthur's note on page 21 and Professor Crank-Pott's diary on pages 16 and 17 should give you some hints.

Pages 26-27
This is easy. They can jump from pillar to pillar and climb over the tree.

Pages 28-29
Try exchanging the last letter of the first word with the first letter of the next word.

Pages 30-31
Find the missing numbers first. Ascending means going up.

Pages 32-33
Arthur's note on page 29 describes the time chart.

Pages 34-35
Find the time door entrance first. Remember the points of the compass:

Pages 36-37
What equipment do both Zack and Jo have? Look at pages 6 and 7.

Pages 38-39
Use Arthur's figures to work out how long it will take Freddie, the Monstermagus and the lava to pass the ledge.

Pages 40-41
Can you spot anything unusual in the picture?

Page 42
Look back through the book at everyone's shoeprints.

Answers

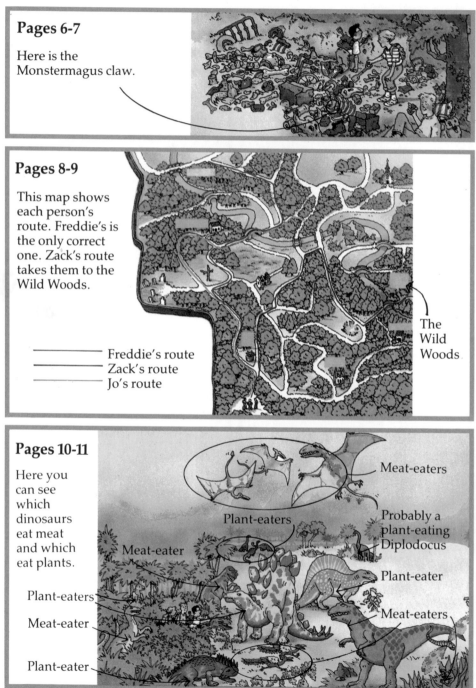

Pages 6-7

Here is the Monstermagus claw.

Pages 8-9

This map shows each person's route. Freddie's is the only correct one. Zack's route takes them to the Wild Woods.

The Wild Woods

———— Freddie's route
———— Zack's route
———— Jo's route

Pages 10-11

Here you can see which dinosaurs eat meat and which eat plants.

Meat-eaters

Plant-eaters

Probably a plant-eating Diplodocus

Meat-eater

Plant-eater

Meat-eaters

Plant-eaters

Meat-eater

Plant-eater

Pages 14-15

Jo has seen five different sets of shoeprints. This means two other people have also travelled backwards in time.

These footprints do not belong to Zack, Jo or Freddie.

Freddie's footprint

Zack's footprint

Jo's footprint

Pages 16-17

This is the page from the diary, when the pieces are put together.

> **AUGUST**
> **MONDAY 20th**
> All the figures work. At long last I've found the secret of the time door again. Recruited a boy called Arthur as my assistant. He's brilliant at sums, but I don't like children at all.
>
> **TUESDAY 21st**
> Making plans. The time door appears on Saturday. I shall travel back 150 million years and steal some dinosaur eggs. Then I shall bring them home and hatch them. I shall cause chaos in the modern world with my little pets.
>
> **WEDNESDAY 22nd**
> Spent the day digging at the dinosaur site in Fossilwood Forest with a lot of silly experts. They think I'm mad, but I'll prove them wrong – I'm a genius!
>
> **THURSDAY 23rd**
> At the site again. Gilbert, my pet python, is a little off-colour. Gave him some special potion. Clumsy Arthur dropped my favourite test tube.
>
> **FRIDAY 24th**
> Success! Fame at last. I have found the skeleton of a real monster of a dinosaur and called it Monstermagus. Arthur was late this morning and he overcooked my swordfish steak. He will suffer for it. Gilbert is better.
>
> **SATURDAY 25th**
> My plan goes ahead today. I shall steal the eggs of the Monstermagus. If my calculations are correct, I will find its nest in a desert clearing near purple poison pools.

Pages 18-19

The man is Professor Crank-Pott. Zack recognizes him from the newspaper photo on page 5, shown below.

Pages 20-21

Freddie has an inflatable air cushion (see pages 6 and 7). They can blow it up and cling on to it. This will keep them afloat as the cave floods. When the water reaches the roof, they can scramble out of the hole at the top.

Pages 22-23

Arthur's trail is marked here in black.

Pages 24-25

The nest is behind this volcano. Arthur's note on page 21 says the nest is South of a blue-capped volcano, South of the swamp. The Professor's diary on pages 16 and 17 says it is in a desert clearing near purple poison pools.

South is directly ahead of Zack

Pages 26-27

The route down the rocky pillars is marked in black.

They climb over this tree.

Pages 28-29

The message is decoded by swapping the last letter of every word with the first letter of the next.

You are very near the nest. Don't worry about the Monstermagus. The Professor's dart will put it to sleep for one hour. You can find the time doors on the Professor's time chart – it's an old, torn roll of paper tied with one red ribbon.

Pages 30-31

Here is the box with the missing numbers added. The buttons marked 2, 4, 6 and 8 will open the lock.

Pages 32-33

This is the only one of the papers that fits Arthur's description on page 29.

Pages 34-35

The compass bearings pinpoint the time doors, marked below.

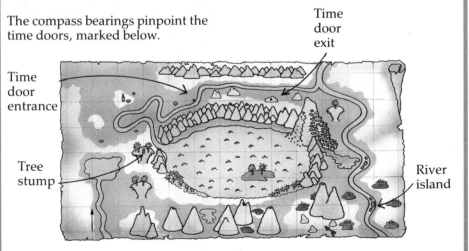

Time door exit

Time door entrance

Tree stump

River island

Pages 36-37

Zack and Jo both have spades which they can use as paddles.

Pages 38-39

Freddie runs four metres a second so he will pass under the ledge in two seconds' time. The lava will reach the ledge, way above him, in three seconds' time, so Freddie is safe.

The Monstermagus will pass under the ledge in four seconds' time. At this point, the lava will be 15 metres from the ground which means it will hit the Monstermagus on the head. The Monstermagus is 15 metres tall (see Zack's newspaper on page 5).

Pages 40-41

Here is the time door.

Through it, you can see St Elmo's Church, shown in the map on pages 8 and 9.

Page 42

Freddie is the only one whose footprint matches the fossil print. The print was made in the soft mud when Freddie was running away from Monstermagus. The volcanic lava preserved his and the dinosaur's footprints, as well as the dinosaur's skeleton. They eventually became fossils (see pages 12 and 13).

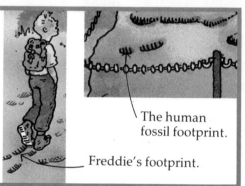

The human fossil footprint.

Freddie's footprint.